Clean Up, Everybody

Provided by:
Conscious Awareness Learning Model - (CALM)

In partnership with:
Children's Board of Hillsborough County
and
Hillsborough Community

by Stacey Sparks • illustrated by Julia Patton

Ken and I were almost done with the big puzzle, but it had two holes. It looked like it was missing teeth.

"Are you sitting on the pieces, Eddie?"
Ken asked. I stood up, but there
were no pieces.

3

"Miss Jan!" we called.
She came over and we
showed her the puzzle.

"This is what happens when we don't clean up," she said. "Things get lost."

Ken and I left the puzzle and took out the trains. "Let's make an oval track," I said.

We did not have enough bendy pieces.

"Miss Jan!" we called again.

When Miss Jan saw our track, she asked everybody to come over to the toy bins.

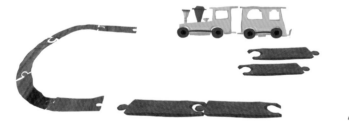

"It's time for a toy treasure hunt!"
she announced. "Let's go through the bins
and make sure everything is in its place."

At first, the hunt was a mess.
Then I finally found toy treasure.

"Look!" I called out.

"The missing puzzle pieces!

They were in the animal bin!"

"I found the bendy tracks," said Ken. "They were mixed in with the blocks!"

Maddie found giraffes in the arts and crafts. Eva found crayons in with the cars.

Jack even found his long-lost dinosaur that he had brought in weeks earlier!

When the toy hunting was over,
we put everything back where
it belonged.

Miss Jan gave us a big smile and asked, "Aren't toys so much more fun when we take care of them?"